Disney's Two-Minute Stories Mickey Mouse and Friends

Eight Funny Adventures With Mickey and His Pals

Cover illustration
by RON DIAS

A GOLDEN BOOK • NEW YORK
Western Publishing Company, Inc., Racine, Wisconsin 53404

 Library of Congress Catalog Card Number: 90-84657 ISBN: 0-307-12193-3/ISBN: 0-307-62193-6 (lib. bdg.) MCMXCII

Mickey and the Beanstalk

High on a hill, overlooking Happy Valley, stood a magnificent castle. In the castle lived the Golden Harp, who sang all day and cast a magic spell of happiness over the land.

But one day the Golden Harp disappeared from the valley. The birds stopped singing and the crops stopped growing. All the people of Happy Valley grew sad and hungry.

"We must do something," said Farmer Donald.

"We'll starve if we don't," added Farmer Goofy.

"I'll sell Bossy the cow and buy some food," said Farmer Mickey.

When Mickey returned, he said, "I have sold the cow for three magic beans."

"Three beans!" cried Donald and Goofy. "We can't live on three beans!" Donald threw the beans on the floor in disgust, where they disappeared into a crack in the floor.

During the night the beans sprouted and began to grow. They grew into a stalk that lifted the farmers' house high into the sky.

When the hungry farmers awoke, Happy Valley was gone! They found themselves in front of a large castle among the clouds. They scampered into the castle and ate and ate from huge platters of food on an enormous table.

"Please help," said a soft voice. "A giant kidnapped me and brought me here to his castle." It was the Golden Harp, locked in a box on the table.

Just then everyone heard the loud footsteps of the giant approaching the table.

"Run!" shouted Mickey to Donald and Goofy. But it was too late to hide!

The giant chased the three farmers around the room until they were cornered. The giant reached down to scoop them up in his hand—but he missed Mickey!

The giant put Donald and Goofy into the box with the Golden Harp. He locked the box and slipped the key into his pocket. Then he sat in his chair and took a nap.

Mickey tiptoed over to the sleeping giant. Carefully, he pulled the key out of the giant's pocket. Then he sneaked back to the box, unlocked it, and lifted out the Golden Harp.

Just as Mickey, Donald, and Goofy were sneaking past the giant, he opened one eye and let out a roar!

The farmers ran as quick as they could, but the giant followed close behind them. Then they jumped on the beanstalk and slid down in a flash. They grabbed a saw and cut the beanstalk down. The giant fell and crashed through the ground, all the way to the center of the Earth.

The Golden Harp began to sing again, and from that time on, Happy Valley has always been happy—thanks to Mickey, Donald, and Goofy!

Some Ducks Have All the Luck

"Today is Daisy's birthday," Donald Duck told his nephews one morning. "I need to get her a better present than the one that lucky Gladstone Gander gives her."

Donald decided to follow Gladstone Gander all over town to see what he was going to buy for Daisy.

Meanwhile, Gladstone Gander was thinking, "I sure hope I get lucky today. I have to come up with a really great present for Daisy." Just then Gladstone found a dollar bill lying on the ground.

"Well, every little bit helps," Gladstone said.

Gladstone soon had a funny feeling that he was being followed. He chuckled when he saw Donald's reflection in a jewelry store window.

"I bet Donald is as worried about Daisy's present as I am," thought Gladstone. "I know how to give him a real scare!"

Gladstone Gander marched into the jewelry store and looked at some diamond bracelets. He held them up, just to make sure Donald saw.

Outside, poor Donald groaned. "That must have been a thousand-dollar bill he just found! Now he's buying Daisy a diamond bracelet. Some ducks have all the luck!" Donald thought. He headed for home with his head down.

Gladstone Gander went home, too, and opened his mail.

"Maybe I've won another contest," Gladstone thought as he tore open an envelope. He read eagerly, "You have won a dinner for two at the grand opening of Chez Swann, the swankiest restaurant in Duckburg.

"My good luck strikes again!" cried Gladstone. "This is the perfect present for Daisy. Donald doesn't have a chance."

When Donald got home, Huey, Dewey, and Louie were waiting for him. "We have a surprise for you, Uncle Donald. We found out what Aunt Daisy wants most for her birthday, and we got it for you to give to her. Let's go!"

Donald and his nephews hadn't been at Daisy's house long when Gladstone Gander appeared at the door.

"Happy birthday, dear Daisy!" Gladstone exclaimed. "How would you like to go with me to the swankiest restaurant in Duckburg?"

"I'd love to, Gladstone," Daisy replied. "But I simply can't leave my darling kitty that Donald just gave me! Why don't you and Donald have my birthday dinner together?" Daisy said, showing them both to the door.

At Chez Swann, Donald lifted his glass and toasted, "To Daisy and her kitty!"

"To Daisy," Gladstone Gander agreed. Then he grumbled, "Your present was the best, Donald! Some ducks have all the luck."

Those Were the Days

Mickey and his nephews Morty and Ferdie were going to have an exciting week. They were to be the caretakers of Founders' Village while Mr. Bumbles was away.

"We know just what to do!" said Morty. "Every morning the horse gets hitched to the surrey. Then when all the people come, we'll take them for a surrey ride around the village."

"Afterward we'll serve homemade lemonade and popcorn," Ferdie said. "We'll make the popcorn on the wood-burning stove. Won't it be fun! A whole week living just the way our grandparents did."

"Those were the days, huh?" Morty said with a chuckle as they started for the stable to hitch up the horse.

But the day didn't start off so well. First, the horse refused to stand still. Then it trotted into the stable and wouldn't come out again. Next, no water came out of the pump when the boys decided to make lemonade.

"Where's the electric juicer?" asked Morty. "And where's the outlet to plug it in?"

"There's no ice. And the woodbox is empty," complained Ferdie.

"There's a woodpile behind the stable," said Mickey. "You know what that means? You're living in the good old days now, and in those days, boys chopped wood."

The boys sighed, but they chopped the wood. Then Mickey made a fire in the old stove. Suddenly, smoke began to billow into the kitchen.

Mickey opened the stove lid. "Water!" he shouted.

But there was no water. The pump didn't work, and of course Mickey could not call the fire department. In the good old days, people didn't have telephones. So Mickey put out the fire with baking soda.

"That does it," said Mickey. "I'm going to town."

Mickey drove away toward town. When he returned, he was followed by a car full of friends—Goofy, Minnie Mouse, Horace Horsecollar, and Clarabelle Cow!

Clarabelle showed Mickey how to use the stove correctly by turning a handle on the stovepipe. This opened the draft so the smoke could go up the chimney. Then she started popping corn.

Minnie found a hand juicer in one of the cupboards and began to make lemonade. Horace Horsecollar carried a pail of water in from the car. He poured water from the pail to the pump, and moved the pump handle up and down. This time the pump gushed water.

Meanwhile, Goofy had talked the horse into getting hitched up to the surrey.

Mickey and the boys were in business!

"The olden days were really good, weren't they?" said Ferdie.

"You bet," said Mickey. "But with friends, any day is good!"

Donald Duck's Toy Sailboat

"There!" said Donald Duck. "At last it's done!"

Donald stood back to look at his toy sailboat. Making it had been a big job. It had taken him all day.

"Building sailboats makes me hungry," Donald said to himself. So he placed his sailboat on the mantel and had a big lunch. Before he could take his toy boat out to the lake, he fell asleep!

Outside Donald's cottage, in the old elm tree, lived two little chipmunks, Chip and Dale.

"I'm hungry," said Chip, rubbing his empty middle.

"Look!" cried Dale.

Chip looked. On a little island out in the middle of the lake stood a great big oak tree weighted down with acorns on every side.

"How can we get to them?" wondered Chip.

"Look in there!" Dale said, pointing through the window of Donald's house. They could see the boat that Donald had made. In no time at all they had the sailboat down and out the door.

Soon Donald woke from his nap. When he saw his sailboat out on the water, he cried, "I'll fix those chipmunks!"

From the pier he cast a little fishing lure that looked just like a nut. It landed beside the toy boat with a plop.

"Look! Look at this!" cried Dale. He pulled in the floating "acorn" and carried it into the hold.

As soon as Chip and Dale went below, Donald pulled the boat back to shore. The chipmunks did not see Donald pouring water into the cabin of the boat.

"Man the pumps!" cried Chip. The two chipmunks pumped out the water while Donald watched and laughed.

"Ha, ha!" laughed Donald. The chipmunks looked up.

"So that's the trouble!" Dale cried.

He saw the "nut" and flung it at Donald so that Donald became tangled in fishing line. Before Donald could free himself and launch his canoe, Chip and Dale sailed the boat to the island and hauled the acorns on board.

"Oh, well," said Donald. "At least I know the sailboat really will sail. Now let's just see what those little fellows do."

Can you guess what the chipmunks did? They stored their nuts in a hollow tree. And then they took Donald's toy sailboat right back and put it where it belonged!

Cowboy Mickey

"Hurry, Mickey," urged Minnie. "I just can't wait to be a cowgirl at the Lucky Star Dude Ranch!"

"I'm excited, too!" Mickey told her. "I've always wanted to learn how to ride a horse!"

Just then Goofy raced in with his suitcase. "Let's go!" he said. "I'm going to learn how to ride and to twirl a lasso so I can perform in the Lucky Star Rodeo."

When the friends arrived at the ranch, they were greeted by the owner. "Call me Cowboy Bob," he said. "I'm going to give you folks some riding lessons." Cowboy Bob held the horses' reins as he helped Mickey, Minnie, and Goofy step up and onto their horses.

"Hey, that wasn't hard at all," bragged Goofy. "Now I'm ready to learn how to lasso."

"Lassoing takes lots of practice," said Cowboy Bob, and he gave Goofy his first lesson.

The next day Mickey and Minnie practiced their riding, while Goofy practiced with his lasso. He tried to rope fences and the Lucky Star sign, but he always ended up roping himself.

Even so, Cowboy Bob said they all could perform in the upcoming rodeo.

The day of the rodeo, Mickey overslept! He got dressed as fast as he could and dashed out the door. "I'm late!" he thought. "I'd better take all the shortcuts I can."

He raced across a field and jumped over a fence.

"Uh-oh," Mickey groaned. "Maybe I shouldn't have jumped over that fence." Mickey had just landed on a bucking bronco in the middle of the rodeo arena!

Everyone cheered as Mickey held tightly to the reins, riding the bronco. "This is fun!" thought Mickey, and he waved his hat to the crowd.

"Ladies and gentlemen," called the rodeo announcer, "Mickey Mouse just broke the ranch record for the longest time riding a bronco." The crowd cheered again.

When Mickey jumped off the bronco, it began to chase him. "What do I do now?" shouted Mickey.

"I'll lasso him for you," yelled Goofy, but he lassoed Mickey instead.

Seeing Mickey all roped up was such a funny sight that even the bucking bronco stopped for a chuckle.

Everybody cheered as Cowboy Bob presented the rodeo ribbons. Minnie won for being the best cowgirl. Mickey won for his bronco riding. And Goofy won for trying to lasso everything in sight!

Donald Duck and the One Bear

Donald Duck was taking something out of the oven when his three nephews walked into the kitchen.

"Those pizzas sure look good," said Huey.

"Two of them do, anyway," added Dewey.

"What's the *other* one?" asked Louie, wrinkling his nose.

"That's my personal favorite," said Donald. "Pineapple and sardines. And there's a pizza with pepperoni on it for Daisy and one with sausage for you boys. Now, don't touch! We'll go get Daisy first, and the pizzas will be cool enough to eat when we get back."

No sooner had they left than a shaggy brown bear came down the street. Something smelled good! When he saw the pizzas sitting on Donald's table, he gave a happy little growl and crawled right through the open window.

The bear tried to pick up a piece of Daisy's pepperoni pizza, but it was too hot. He picked up a piece of the boy's sausage pizza, but it was too cold. Then he tried Donald's pineapple and sardine pizza, and it was just right. So he ate it all up!

With his tummy full of pizza, the bear lumbered upstairs for a nap. First he tried Huey's bed, but it was too small. So he tried stretching from Dewey's bed to Louie's, but he sagged in the middle. Finally he found Donald's bed, and that was just right! He snuggled under the covers and fell fast asleep.

When Donald, Daisy, and the boys came back, Donald proudly pointed to the pizzas. But Daisy could only cry, "Somebody's been trying to eat my pizza!"

"Somebody's been eating *our* pizza!" exclaimed the boys.

"Hey!" shouted Donald. "Somebody's been eating my pizza— and has eaten it all up! I'm going to get to the bottom of this!" He charged up the stairs, with Daisy and the nephews following nervously.

"Hey!" shouted Huey from the doorway of his room. "Somebody's been sleeping in my bed!"

"And my bed!" added Dewey.

"Mine too!" said Louie.

"Help!" screamed Donald from his room.

Daisy and the boys ran down the hall and found Donald hiding behind the dresser.

"Here's the culprit," Daisy said, laughing.

"Wow! Can we keep him, Uncle Donald?" asked the boys.

Donald poked his head out from behind the dresser. He tried to act brave. "C-Certainly n-not," he said.

The doorbell rang. Donald hurried out of the room to answer the door. A worried-looking little man stood at the door.

"I'm sorry to bother you," he said, "but I don't know what's happened to my Pizza—"

"We've been wondering that ourselves," Donald interrupted. "Mine got all eaten up, and—"

"No, no, no!" the man said frantically. "Pizza is my pet bear! You see, I own Charlie's Pizza, and our slogan is 'When you're as hungry as a bear, eat Charlie's Pizza.' Get it?"

"I get it," Donald said. "But I'd be happier if *you'd* get your *bear*. He's upstairs."

Charlie ran upstairs yelling, "Pizza! Pizza!" Pizza was glad to see Charlie, and followed him out to his truck. Then the doorbell rang. It was Charlie again, holding three boxes. "Here's a reward for finding my bear," he said. "I hope you like them—they're pineapple and sardine, Pizza's favorite!"

Huey, Dewey, and Louie stared glumly at the pizzas, but Donald grinned. "I liked that bear from the moment I saw him," he said. "Now, let's eat!"

Mickey Mouse and the Great Lot Plot

Morty and Ferdie were shocked. The vacant lot they played on was for sale! Where were they going to play ball now?

"I'm going to buy that lot," said a voice behind them. It was Uncle Scrooge McDuck. "It's right next to my money bin, and it's the best place for my new business—SCROOGE'S PERFECTLY PLANTED, PICKED AND PROCESSED, PATENTED PICKLED PRESERVES!"

Mickey Mouse and the boys followed Uncle Scrooge to his money bin. "Won't you please think it over, Uncle Scrooge?" Mickey asked. "The children really need a place to play."

"No!" answered Uncle Scrooge. "My mind is made up!"

Before Mickey quite knew what he was saying, he announced, "I'm going to buy the lot, and I'll make it into a playground for everyone to enjoy."

Scrooge laughed so hard that he rolled off a pile of money. "You'll never be able to afford it!" he said.

"Don't worry, Uncle Mickey!" said Morty and Ferdie. "We'll earn the money you need. Our friends will be happy to help, too!"

For the next month everybody was busy. Goofy walked dogs, Daisy Duck and Minnie baked pies and cakes for Morty and Ferdie to sell, and Donald Duck and his nephews washed cars. Mickey was the busiest of all, helping with everything.

At the end of the month Mickey counted up all the money that everyone had earned. It came to exactly five hundred dollars. That wasn't much, and Mickey was worried!

Later that day Scrooge walked happily down the street and stopped in front of the empty lot. There were Morty and Ferdie.

"Here, catch!" Morty shouted. He threw the ball to Scrooge.

Before he knew it, Uncle Scrooge was out on the empty lot playing a fast game of baseball.

"Well, Uncle Scrooge," said Morty, "now do you see what's so great about a playground?"

But Uncle Scrooge only said, "Humph!"

The next day Mickey and his friends noticed a new sign on the lot. It said: SOLD TO SCROOGE McDUCK.

With sad faces, they all turned to leave, but Scrooge appeared and shouted, "Wait here a few minutes. I have a surprise for you!"

Soon workmen began to arrive. They lifted swings and slides into place! They started to dig a swimming pool! In the corner, they marked the lines for a baseball diamond!

Weeks later the park opened and the first game was ready to begin. Scrooge McDuck was given the honor of hitting the very first ball.

"Hurray!" the crowd cheered as the ball soared through the air.

The cheer was cut short by the tinkling of glass. The ball had crashed through a window in Scrooge's money bin!

But Uncle Scrooge was already on his way to first base. "It's only glass," he shouted over his shoulder. "But did you see that? I do believe I hit a home run!"

Mickey Mouse Heads for the Sky

Mickey Mouse was taking a flying lesson with his teacher, "Ducky" Lindy. "I can't believe it," Mickey cried after a little while. "I'm actually flying a plane!"

Mickey took lesson after lesson. He wanted to be the best pilot ever.

One day Minnie said, "Mickey, I haven't seen you at all lately. Won't you come swimming with me?"

"I can't," Mickey told her. "I'm much too busy learning how to fly."

"Oh," said Minnie sadly. She went to the swimming pool without him.

A few days later Goofy asked Mickey to play baseball with him. "You're the best pitcher I know," said Goofy.

"I'd really like to play," said Mickey, "but today I'm going to learn to fly upside-down!"

Mickey flew upside-down perfectly.

"Good for you," said Ducky. "Soon you'll be ready for your first solo flight."

"Hey, Mickey!" said Donald Duck a few days later. "Today we're having the last picnic of the summer. Don't forget to come."

"I'll try," Mickey told Donald, "but today's the day of my first solo flight. If I do everything right, I'll be an official pilot."

Later that day Mickey was nervous as he prepared to fly alone, but his takeoff was perfect. He flew the plane higher and higher. He did all the special flying tricks he had learned. He tried his best, and he did it all just right.

"You pass the test!" Ducky told him over the radio. "Now, why don't you spend the afternoon up in the sky?"

"Thanks!" said Mickey. "I feel so proud! I wish my friends could be here with me."

Mickey flew over the tennis courts, but all he saw were nets. He flew by the swimming pool, but all he saw was water.

"Where can everyone be?" Mickey wondered. Suddenly, below him, he saw a big banner. The banner said, WE MISS MICKEY!

And under the banner were Minnie, Donald, Goofy, Daisy, and Pluto.

Mickey landed his plane next to the banner.

"What a terrific message!" he told his friends. "I've missed all of you, too. I guess I got a little carried away with my flying lessons. But I'm glad I learned to fly, because I'm going to take each of you for a ride in my plane!"